Love OF SOULS

Love OF SOULS

SANDY DONALDSON

THE REGENCY
PUBLISHERS

Copyright © 2023 by Sandy Donaldson.

All rights reserved. No part of this book may be reproduced in any form or by any electronic or mechanical means, including information storage and retrieval systems, without permission in writing from the author and publisher, except by reviewers, who may quote brief passages in a review.

ISBN: 978-1-962313-53-7 (Paperback)
ISBN: 978-1-962313-54-4 (Hardcover)
ISBN: 978-1-962313-52-0 (E-book)

Some characters and events in this book are fictitious and products of the author's imagination. Any similarity to real persons, living or dead, is coincidental and not intended by the author.

Book Ordering Information

The Regency Publishers, US
521 5th Ave 17th floor NY, NY10175

Phone Number: (315)537-3088 ext 1007
Email: info@theregencypublishers.com
www.theregencypublishers.com

Printed in the United States of America

Acknowledgements

I would like to especially thank Debbie Townsend, for standing by me when I have writer's block.

I would like to thank my children for standing by me while I write this book.

Chapter 1

I'm not what or who you think I am. My name is Ilayi. I have been told that I am not human. I have also been told that I am not of my race either. I am one of a kind among both races. Sitting on this roof top seeing humans and vampires running the streets below is hard when you know that you don't belong with either of them.

I'm sure that you have probably heard stories about vampires being in brotherhoods that protect our kind. I'm sure that you have also heard that every mate to these brothers give birth to only males. Well, it just so happens that a female is born every five thousand years. I have to say that this makes me kind of special for both kinds.

My parents were both purebred vampires. They were shocked that I was a girl when I was born some three hundred years ago. They were killed by crones trying to keep me alive. I was eight when my parents were slain down in cold blood.

There was a man that I remember being around when I was little. He called me the chosen one. I never really knew what that meant. As I watch this man now from this rooftop, I still have images of him from my youth that fill my head. This man, Marcus, is the leader of the Marked Brotherhood. The brotherhood carries a mark on their neck that looks like two horseshoes inverted within each other. Marcus is a vicious male in battle. I have witnessed this from above on these very rooftops. The brothers never know that I am around during their battles. I watch without them knowing, hoping that I am someday needed. There are five members of the

Marked Brotherhood. Marcus is the leader, Craven is someone you really don't want to know, Kage is a heartthrob, Tate is very secretive, and last but not least is Devin who has been through hell. These guys are the closest thing that I know of to a family. I have watched them for the past hundred years.

Chapter 2

I watch Marcus from the opposite side of the club. Other vampires are not able to detect my presence. He is over six feet tall with black hair that comes to his shoulders and blue eyes that send chills down my spine. He is sitting at the table in the shadows of the VIP room upstairs. I can see that the two women with him are trying to seduce him. I see his hands running over their bodies as he leans in to bite one the girls on the neck. She moans a little to the touch of his warm lips against her neck. She has no idea what he is doing to her. When he pulls away from her neck, she will remember nothing that he has done to her. For some reason there is something that draws me to this man. He realizes that someone is watching him and turns around to search the club. He sees me standing across the club leaning against a wall. The look upon his face tells me that he is surprised to see me and he is not sure that it is really me that he is seeing. I slip out of the club when he turns around to get up from his table of guests.

The heat of the summer night is so hot when it hits me in the face. I move so fast down the sidewalk that by the time he is outside of the club, I am gone from his sight. I watch him from a nearby rooftop. He is always so sure that it is me that he sees. My skin tingles with energy when I am close to him. I can see the doubt on his face as he searches for me down the nearby alleys. I have only let him see me three times now. I am getting sloppy with him. He makes my heart race when I am near him.

I turn the locks to my condo downtown. There is very little furniture in my place. There is only a sofa and some chairs in the living room. My kitchen is really only for books since I don't have to eat if I don't want to. There are bags of blood in the frig from a nearby blood bank. I only take what I need to survive. My bedroom has a king size bed with black satin sheets. All my windows have steel blinds that lower at sunrise. This place is lonely to me. It's where I live but it is far from being called a home to me.

Marcus is still a little confused about what we saw in the club when he gets back to the compound. Was it really her? Was it really Ilayi after all this time? I saw the little girl that I once knew in this woman's face. This woman's eyes were so remarkably similar to hers. Those green eyes just looked right through me with no depth what so ever. I never even felt her presence in the club. She was so beautiful to me. The long black braid that ran down her back was perfect. Her body was of a goddess yet strong. She had skin kissed by the sun which is something that I could never figure out how she could accomplish. Vampires are deathly scared of sunlight. Her father was my closest friend. He made me promise to keep her safe from harm if something should happen to him. When I had brought her to my home after the deaths of her parents, I saw that a part of her soul had died that day. The tears that ran down her face ripped my soul in half. When I got up the next night, she was gone from the upstairs compound. Seeing her tonight placed images of when she was happy with her family burning in my mind. I didn't even hear Kage coming up behind me until his hand landed on my shoulder.

"Dude, you like you saw a ghost. What's up my man? Is everything ok out there tonight?"

"Yeah man, everything is ok tonight."

"Are you sure? Were you headed to the control room?"

"Yeah, just give me a minute."

"Okay, I'll tell Tate that you will be a few minutes and for us to wait."

"Thanks Kage."

When Kage left, I leaned against the wall and took deep breaths as my body shook thinking about her. Man, what the hell is going on tonight? When I got to the control room all the brothers were already there.

Chapter 3

Tate looked at me with grief as I came in. he had six computer monitors lined up on the wall in front of him, each displaying a crime scene.

"What the hell is that?"

"There was another round of killings last night on the upper side. The local police department thinks it's a serial killer as always."

"Those fools couldn't get their ass out of a bag with a hole in it" laughed Kage.

Craven, who was standing against the far wall, said "The killings are getting worst, Marcus. This is the third one this week alone."

"What the hell are we going to do about it, Marcus?" said Devin stretched out on a chair.

Marcus started pacing the room, running things through his head. "Tomorrow night we spread our detail further out. This has to stop now before any more killings occur."

Ilayi was watching the news when a special report came against the screen. The blonde woman was talking about more killings on the upper side. Damn it, she thought, I've missed another one. These crones are really pissing me off. The blood in my veins boils with the thought of more innocent people being killed. I change my clothes and I am out the door within a minute. I have to see that crime scene. I have to be sure that it was crones who did this. The sun is so damn hot during the day. Yes, you heard me right, the sun. I have the ability to stay out in sunlight for about four hours without my skin blistering up. This is thanks to the female being born every five thousand years. It's my gift like all vampires have. This ability allows me to be outside in the daylight for a while. The trip up state is going to push me getting back in time so I won't burn. When I arrive at the scene, the law enforcement is already long gone. I take a deep breath of the blood that has been spilled. The four victims were terrified when they were killed. The smell of crone blood makes my stomach hurt. I leave the scene with nothing much to go on. I went to the morgue to see the bodies. The family apparently didn't know what was happening until it was too late. The face of the little girl brings a pain to my stomach. I grab my waist trying to shake the pain. It's now getting late and my time is almost up. As I stepped outside into the heat, my body started aching. I have run out of time. I need to find shelter from the sun. I break into a warehouse and wait until dusk.

When it was dark enough for me to be safe I headed home. I got home feeling the heat on my skin. I turned on the shower and stepped under the cool water. Steam came off my skin as the cool water hit it. My eyes turn amber and my fangs come out as the hiss escapes from my lips. After my shower I hit the streets for the night. I head to Moonlights, the club nearby. Two guys run into me when I turn the corner of Maple Street. When I look up, I see the amber of their eyes. I quickly take my blades out of my side holster. The crones turn around with their fangs showing and hissing at me. I was ready for a good fight when the first one came charging at me. I brought my blades up just in time to catch this crone across the throat. He screamed with pain at the contact of my blades. The sliver blade burned when it touched his skin. I slam the blade in his heart. The other crone slammed into me when my blade hit the other in the chest. He knocked me against the wall. I threw him off and took his head off with my blade. As the crones turned to dust, one of the brothers rounded the corner. I knew he was a brother by the mark on the side of his neck. He scares the shit out of me most of the time. He's six feet and a half with pure evil coming from his muscled body. His eyes shot to me as he looked at the cones that I just took out. The next thing I knew a 9mm was in my face.

My amber eyes burn with fire. My fangs shoot out as a loud hiss leaves my lips. Craven just stood there looking at me with surprised expression on his face. He looks down for a half of a second at the bodies on the ground. When he looks up again I am gone. Running for my life, I thought for sure Craven would come after me. When I reach the club I go in and head straight for the back where the VIP section is. I set down at a booth and took a deep breath. My body was running crazy from the adrenalin of the situation.

Chapter 4

Close to daylight, after my patrol, I head back to the compound. I still have the face of the woman in the alley in my head. What the hell was she thinking fighting those crones? She had actually put herself in danger killing them. I was shocked when I saw the amber eyes and fangs. What the fuck was that? There was never been a pureblood female vampire that I know of. She sure in the hell wasn't a crone. The muscled body that she had and the way that she moved in battle was like a warrior or a brother. Craven stepped into the control room to report in on tonight's patrol with the rest of the brothers.

"Craven, any luck out there tonight?"

"I killed three crones tonight," *God should I tell them about the woman?* "I ran across two more that were already dead."

"Dude, I am telling you that someone beat me to it. I thought it was one of your guys."

Marcus looked at Craven searching for any reason not to believe him. Marcus and Craven had been closed for about eight hundred years now. It's not like him to keep shit from me, he thought.

Craven looked around the room and let a curse out under his breath, "I'm out of here."

My head is so damn crazy lately. What the hell was I thinking out here tonight? Standing in the hot shower, I let the water run down my body as my head is still reeling from the battle of the two crones. I can still feel the painful dark side of Craven on my skin. That brother has one hell of a dark side. A knock on my door brings me back to reality. I get out and slide my black silk robe on as I go to the door. I placed one of my blades behind my back since I'm not expecting anyone. I look in the peek hole and see it's the guy next door, Dalton. I slide my blade to my side just in case of trouble and open the door for him. I have seen him in the hall a few times. Every time I see him he makes me breathless, he makes my core heat up.

"Hey Dalton, what's up?" OMG! Seeing him standing there with no shirt on and those muscles ripping out everywhere is making my skin tingle. His blonde hair and blue eyes take my breath away. "Dalton, why don't you come in?" My body is still so hot from the battle earlier. It makes me want to strip him down and take advantage of him right here in my doorway. He smiles at me like he knows what I'm thinking and heart stops instantly. "Would you like something to drink?" I open the frig to get a beer out for him. When I turn around he is so close to me that I can feel the heat from his body against mine.

"Ilayi, why do you always assume I want a beer when I come here? You know I never drink it."

He touches my cheek with his hands and caresses my cheek with his thumb. My body temperature rises to his touch. His lips are warm against mine. He kisses me softly, teasing my lips with his tongues as I open up and welcome him in. His kiss becomes more rapid as his hands slide to my breasts. He slides the front of my robe open and touches my hard nipple with his fingers. He starts down my neck and shoulders with small kisses. He reaches my nipples with his warm mouth making me moan with excitement. I feel my eyes burning with amber as he touches me. He slides one hand down to my waist and then lowers it to my hot core. He plays with my clit and it brings me to the edge of my first orgasm that rocks my body. I can feel his sex against my hips. I know he wants me as bad as I want him.

He kisses my stomach and then moves to my inner thighs kissing more as he makes his way to my core. *Oh God! Yes!* As he reaches my core with his mouth, his name slips through my fangs that have formed now. I'm glad it's dark in my apartment so that he can't see my vampire features. My fingers run through his blonde hair as he licks and sucks on my core. I feel another climax coming. My hips are moving with him as another orgasm reaches me. I scream his name out as my body shakes from the orgasm. My legs feel weak from the multiple orgasms. He comes back to my mouth with a hot kiss sliding his tongue in to meet mine. I wrap my legs around him as he carries me to my bed. His body is so hot above mine as they touch slightly.

"Dalton, I want you inside me now. Please! I need to feel you in me."

He moans loudly to my command. He slides his jeans off and then slides his sex between my legs rubbing the outside of my core. He slides into my core with one powerful stroke. I moan loudly when he fills me fully with his sex. My core stretches to welcome his entire sex. He begins with slow strokes in and out of my core. I dig my fingers into his shoulders has he gets faster and harder with his strokes. Another orgasm comes over me. I feel his body tighten under my fingers, I know that he is close to his own orgasm. He moans loudly as his orgasm rushes inside my wet core, sending me over to another orgasm. Both of our bodies shake as we release together. He slides off of me and lies beside me. He pulls me into his arms.

"Ilayi, do you know what the hell you do to me?"

I keep my head down against his chest trying to calm my emotions down so that my vampire feature will go away. He kisses the top of my head as he strokes my arms softly. I know that I shouldn't be with him because he is human.

Chapter 5

I wake up the next morning with Dalton gone from my bed. I hear the shower in the bathroom running. I can't help the smile that comes across my face from the thought of last night's sex and of who is in my shower. I slide off the bed and head to the bathroom. The sight of him through the glass door makes my throbbing body want more. He turns around and sees me standing there. I slide the door open and step inside. Damn it, my body aches just seeing him under the water that is running off his tanned body. He braces me in a kiss and tells me good morning. Seeing his sex harden against my stomach makes me moan his name out. He just smiles at me and pulls me to him. His mouth running over my body sends tingles all over my body. He turns me around and places me against the wall. I arch my body to meet his sex. We both moan at the impact of his sex sliding in my core. We make love for the next two hours. When I wake up again, he is gone. It's already dark again.

I grab a shower and dress in my leathers before I head out for the night. I am sitting on the rooftop near the club from the other night when I see one of the brothers in an alley with four crones. I can smell fresh blood from a human. I drop off the building landing with no noise. My body is all muscle but light as well. I come up behind one of the crones and slice his head off before anyone knows I'm here. I turn to attack the other one with my blades when something knocks me to the ground. A crone came through a door from the building next to me. I turned around and stabbed him in the chest with a dagger. I got up and stared to fight again when my blades hit another set of blades. My eyes widen when I realize it is Marcus's sword that I hit. He pushes me against the wall asking me who the hell I am. Our hands touch sending electric currents through my body. His face looks just like I remember when I was young girl. The expression on his face is strange to me. He is trying to figure out who I am. He whispers Ilayi from his lips. I smile at him knowing that this is not going to be good. He lowers his sword to his side.

"Is it really you after all this time Ilayi?"

"Hello Marcus, it's been a long time hasn't it?"

He pulls me into a strong embrace and whispers in my ear, "I thought you were dead all this time. It was you that I saw the other night in the club wasn't it?"

I have all these feelings swarming inside. When we touched earlier I felt something go through my body, my blood, from her. "What in the hell are you doing out here like this? Fuck, it's really you!" Looking at her now makes my heart hurt. Ilayi agreed to come back to the compound with me figure out what's going on with these killings. It wasn't easy getting her to come back with me. When we return to the compound I sense that she is nervous about being back here again. I pull up to the gates and put my code in and wait for Tate to open the gates. She sits by me so quiet. I'm amazed from the sight of her now. I see the little girl that she used to be. Now I see the strong woman that she has grown into. She doesn't need my protection now. That sends a little pain through me knowing that she never actually needed me. As we walk through the halls to the control room, I see her in different ways. Some of which give me feelings that I shouldn't have any right to feel. The glass door opens to the control room revealing a whole network system with Tate at the wheel.

"Marcus my man, we have . . ." The look on his face was hard. "Who in the fuck is this?"

He scans a look over Ilayi. "Tate, this is none of your business right now. What in the fuck do you have for me?"

"Well, I just got a report that the same thing is happening in other places in the world, not just here in New York."

Tate brings the reports up on screen for me to see. "Damn it, we have to get a fucking grip on this. Do we know someone in England can help with this?"

"Kage is from that area, I will check to see if he has contacts over there."

Chapter 6

Craven, Kage, and Devin came in from the night patrol about half an hour before sunrise.

We passed Marcus and a woman with long black hair and extremely built in the hall while we were headed to control room to report in from the night's activities.

"Craven, who in the fuck is that with Marcus?"

"Kage, I'm sure that it's none of our damn business since she's with Marcus."

I couldn't help but hear a hiss slip from my lips when I passed her in the hall. She stopped and looked at me with fire in her eyes. The fire that burned in my veins from seeing her again made my body ache. The look that she gave me was something from a nightmare. I guess I deserved that though for what happened the other night in the alley. She had surprised me by being there when I turned into the alley after those crones. She had handled herself with warrior skills. I have never seen a woman move like that. When we arrived at the control room I asked Tate, "who in the fuck is that woman with Marcus? He has no fucking business bringing anybody in this compound."

"Well, Craven, I guess Marcus can do what the fuck he wants to do, since he is leader of the Marked Brotherhood."

Marcus led me down a hall to a guest room. In the hallway we passed the brother that I ran into the other night in the alley. I stopped when I heard a hiss come from him. When I turned around, I met the eyes of Craven. They were fiery with amber. He is the one with strong dark side. When I looked closer at him I thought I saw something else in his eyes. I had a feeling that he was different from anyone else there. When we got to my quarters, Marcus told me that if I needed anything to just dial one on the phone and it would go straight to Tate in the control room. I thanked Marcus again for letting me stay until nightfall. He told me to stay as long as I would like. I looked at the room when he left. There was sitting area with a fireplace, a huge bathroom off from the bedroom, and a huge bed with red satin sheets. I stretched out across the bed to relax and think about the strange feeling that was pulling me here. I guess I had fallen asleep when a knock on the door came. I headed for the door telling Marcus I didn't need anything else. When I opened the door, Craven was standing there instead.

"Oh hey, is there something that I can help you with?"

"What the fuck do you think you are doing here?"

His voice was so deep that I could barely understand anything he said. Just the sound of his voice sent chills through my veins. "Why should it be any of your business? I am here because I want to be here."

The mark on the side of his neck turned fiery red. He stormed inside my room demanding me to leave. I was standing my ground telling him to go straight to hell when I felt his lips on mine. I pulled away and was surprised that what I saw in his eyes wasn't fire. His eyes glowed with amber. His mark stared changing colors to purples, reds, and violets, the colors of sexual attraction. I felt an attraction deep in my veins pulling me to him. I know he should leave but I can't get the words to come out of my mouth to tell him to leave. What in the hell is wrong with me? I have a connection with Dalton but this is something different. I can't really explain these feeling inside me telling me to never let this male out of my sight. I placed my finger tips across the symbol on his neck to feel them. I had heard that they are marking of their families. He moans when I touch the beautiful symbol on is neck. It feels like energy passing through my veins from just being near him.

I don't know what the hell drew me to her door. Something inside me told me that I should be with her forever. There is something different about this female, something I have never seen before. She fights like a warrior. She is intelligent, sexy, and strong. What the hell are these feelings inside my veins? I hate feeling this way. I have never let anyone get close to me after my family was slaughtered by those fucking crones. All I can think about is getting to her room. When she opens the door, the look on her face is shock. I know I shouldn't be here at this female's door. Before I could stop myself, I lased out something so damn stupid. This female got right back in my face. I have never had anyone get in my face without killing them. This female is all in my face telling me to get the fuck out of her room and yet I can't seem to move from her. Damn it, this female is driving me fucking crazy. I pressed my lips to hers without thinking. Her soft lips tasted so fucking good to me. She pulled away from me in a hurry. The look that she gave me was confusion, shock, and worry all in one. What the hell was I thinking? Then she touched the symbol on my neck. Her touch was so soft and gentle to me. I grabbed her face with my hands and pressed my lips against hers again. This time she didn't pull away from me. She opened her mouth to welcome my tongue to explore her anyway I wanted. I felt the heat rise between us. Fuck, what's happening to me with this female? She wrapped her arms around my neck and pulled me closer. A loud moan rose from my throat as my fangs extended out. I led my mouth across her cheek, down her neck, her collar bone next, and then something happened, she stopped me. I looked in her eyes to see what was wrong. Her eyes glowing with amber. We shouldn't be doing this. I kissed her again while I slide my hands under her black shirt. Hell, she wasn't wearing any underclothes. My cock went rock hard against my leathers. It's straining to get loose from the cage it's in. she sighed when I touched her firm breast. I left her mouth and went straight to her breasts. I took her shirt off with one quick movement. Her nipples got hard from the touch of my hand. When I took her nipple in my mouth, I heard a small growl coming from her. I wanted even more of her body close to me. I picked her up and pressed her to the wall. Her core was so fucking hot against my cock. I took her black leather pants off in one ripped her panties off with my fangs. She moaned my name when I went ape fucking crazy on her core. She held on to my shoulders and screamed when the orgasm hit her hard. I took my leathers off with one hand and slide her down to meet my hard cock. She screamed loud when I put my whole cock in her core with one full shove. Her walls tightening around my cock as I thrust in and out of her core. She had another orgasm when I stared fucking her harder. She leaned down and whispered in my ear, "Craven fuck me harder." I had to obey this female with my whole body. I let out a loud growl and pressed her hard against the wall and fucked her harder and faster than I ever have in my life. We both screamed loud when our orgasm came together as one. She fell against me and laid her head on my shoulders as I took her to the bed. We had sex for the rest of the day.

Chapter 7

All of the brothers were in the control room when I came in. I froze when hisses from the brothers came out when I entered the room. Marcus was pacing the floor trying to figure out what to do about the situation in England. I heard Kage say something about how he could go and take a look around there. That he would be gone for a few days and handle things there. Tate was trying to get more information about the killings there. There had been another attack there on a community close to Kage's family. Devin was telling him no fucking way was he going alone with these crones. Craven was standing over a map that was on the table in the middle of the room. He didn't even look up when I came into the room. I said that I could go with Kage to England, two fighters would be better than one. Everyone stopped and looked at me. The brothers just realized I was in the room. Devin said "What the fuck is she doing here and who in the fuck is she?"

I started to say that my name was Ilayi when Marcus cut me off. "There is no fucking way that you are going anywhere outside this compound."

The fire in Marcus's face was a surprise to me. I told him to mind his own fucking business, that he didn't have any control over me. The brothers growled across the room. "Nobody talks to Marcus like that" said Devin.

Marcus turned and got control of the brothers. "This is Ilayi, she is a purebred."

All the brothers started talking all at once. Craven looked up at me with concern, fire, and guilt in his eyes.

"You're a what?" Craven whispered.

Marcus was the one that started explaining everything to the brothers. All the brothers went silent at once. They just stood there looking at me like I was some kind of alien. Hell, maybe I was a damn alien.

"That is the reason that she shouldn't go with me to England."

"Ilayi, are you sure that you want to do this?"

"If it takes these sons of a bitch out and stops the killing, then yes I want to go England. When this is over I will go my way and you will go yours, agreed?"

"I can't do that Ilayi."

"Marcus, promise me that you will let me go when we are done."

"Tate, do it, make the agreement."

Tate started pushing buttons on the keyboards. "Okay, I have arrangements for you to leave tomorrow night."

Chapter 8

On the way to the private airstrip, Craven wouldn't speak or look at me. He and Kage were discussing the mission in England.

"Kage, are you sure we can trust your contact in England?"

"Yeah man, Antonio is cool. He will meet us at the airport and we can stay at his place while we are there. Antonio is part of the England Primal Government. He will treat us right and do right by the brothers."

When Craven looked back in the rear view mirror, I saw a little regret and fire in his eyes. I started to say something but then he looked away like he was hurt by me somehow. We didn't bond when we were together today. OH MY GOD, was the sex damn good. I wasn't expecting him to be so passionate with me since he is the one who has the dark side to him.

When we arrived at the airstrip, we got out of the SUV and started getting the gear out of the back. Craven grabbed my hand when I leaned in to get my weapon bag. "You know you have a lot of fucking explaining to do when you get back. You damn well better be coming back too."

We held each other's eyes for a few minutes until yelled at me to hurry up. At the door of the plane I looked back to see him again and noticed he was already leaving. I don't know why I have the need for this ruthless brother that I just met.

The flight was long. I had all these things running around in my head that I couldn't explain. Had I really provoked Marcus into letting me come on this mission? Why did I think that I had to prove myself to the brothers? I've never had the need to worry about someone else's approval before. I feel so tired sitting here trying to figure out this mess I'm in with the brothers. The thought of Craven and me together crosses my mind. Had I really gave in to this rude and hatred brother? I dosed off to sleep I guess. Kage woke me up a few hours later telling me that we were at the airstrip. The images of me and Craven in the bed were still in my mind when Kage asked me what was wrong.

"Ilayi, what the fuck are you smiling at? This is not some parade we headed to." "Oh . . . sorry . . .jusking thinking."

A small curve came up at the edges of Kage's mouth. "That's what I thought you would say, Ilayi."

Chapter 9

The door opened and I saw a huge male standing beside the black SUV. Kage greeted the male as Antonio braced him in a hard handshake.

"Brother, how have you been? I see that England has been well to you."

"Kage, how the hell are you?"

"You know what they say, if you can't enjoy life you shouldn't be in it."

"Come on, I have everything ready for you at the compound."

"Antonio, I want you to meet Ilayi. She is a friend of the brotherhood and is protected by us also."

Antonio took my hand and kissed it. "Welcome to England my dear."

"Thank you, Mr. Ayes, for having me."

"Please call me Antonio. Kage, you didn't tell me that she was so beautiful when we spoke and told me that you were bringing a guest."

"I know how you are brother, with the ladies."

The SUV had tinted the windows so dark that you couldn't see out without vampire sight. The driver had no problems driving us back to the compound.

"So kage, what kind of business is here for you and the lovely Ilayi?"

"I told you the business over the phone yesterday, that we are looking for someone here. Antonio, how many killings have they been so far here? I know of the two that were reported but I think that there are probably some that they think are not important or do not obtain to this."

"I know there have been four others from what I have gathered from my other sources."

When we arrived at the compound, it was like nothing I have ever seen. There were iron gates with security codes and cameras. There was a strong force that surrounded the compound. The SUV pulled into a garage to the back of the house. Antonio and Kage got out of the SUV and started toward the door. I just stood looking in amazement at the sight of the compound. Kage turned around and gave me that OMG! Smile and came to where I was standing by the SUV. He asked me if everything was alright. I gave him a smile and told him that I have never seen anything like this place in my life. "Is this where you grew up at?"

Of course, he is looking at me like I have completely lost my mind. "Well yeah but nobody knows that Ilayi, not even the brotherhood. Come on let's go in and I'll show you around. The inside is a lot better than the garage."

He takes my hand and leads me inside the house. We step inside and it takes my breath away. The white marble floors were so beautiful. The walls were a soft cream color. All the windows had long beautiful dark drapes hanging from them. You could barely see the steel shutters behind the drapes. I had never been in a place like this. I can remember my parents' place a little from my childhood and I always thought it was beautiful, but this place takes my breath away just being in it.

There are stairs that come off both sides of the entrance room. I look up as a woman's voice caught my attention from the staircase. A woman with long blonde curly hair to her waist was coming down the staircase. Her skin was sun kissed like mine so I know that she can stay in the sun like me but I get the sense that she is not like vampires. I can tell that she is pampered a lot in her lifestyle. She has high cheek bones. She is beautiful like the place that she lives in. she is drawn tight. When the woman reached us she asked Antonio if he was not going to introduce his friends to her. The surprised look on Antonio's face told me that she was an unexpected guest in the house.

"Angel, this is Ilayi and Kage, and my brother. They are here from the states on business."

"Angel, it's a pleasure to meet you" Ilayi said.

"Thank you."

The color of her eyes matched the color of her gown. Her eyes were like looking at the ocean waves first thing in the morning. Kage just looked at her. I put my hand on his arm and told her that he was very tired from our trip. He glanced at me like he was just realizing that I was there.

Antonio broke the silence, "Well please, let me show you to your rooms and we can meet up later for last meal."

I pulled Kage along with me toward the stairs. Antonio led us down the long hallway lined with bust statues of different males. We came to the fourth door and Antonio opened the door for me and said "I hope this is acceptable, if you need anything just press zero on the phone and that will send you straight to Henry."

"Thank you Antonio, I'm sure it will be fine." Ilayi told them both goodnight and went inside the room.

Chapter 10

The room has dark tan walls, deep red drapes from the windows, and a king bed with black silk sheets. The floor was white marble with red and black marking on the squares. I went into the bathroom and started the shower. The way that Kage had acted really bothered me. What was his problem down there I wondered. I got in the shower, I leaned forward and let the hot water run down my head and back. It had been a very long day. Things started going through my head. Images of Dalton, Craven, and Kage started running through my mind. The scene from downstairs was running through my head also. What was that all about? Why had Kage acted like that? I can feel Craven on my skin. Why does he seem so close to me? It makes my body ache for him. I can even smell him on me. Had he marked me somehow with me not knowing it? I turned off the water and slid the door open. I heard someone knocking on my door. I put on the red bathrobe and went to the door. I opened it with Kage standing there looking at me. He smiled that OMG! Smile at me and stepped inside my room.

"Sure, come on in! Can I help you with something?"

"I was hoping to go in to town tonight to check things out. So I was wondering if you want to ride with me."

"Yeah, give me five minutes to get dressed."

I went to my bag to get ready. Kage told me to wait a minute and went to my closet. He pulled out a red dress for me to wear.

"Hell No! I don't do dresses Kage. Why do you think that I would ever wear that?"

He smiled and my body felt like it just melted to the floor. "I will see you in thirty minutes Ilayi."

He left my room still smiling like he had just won the war or something. When he shut the door, I couldn't help me but smile a little at what he had picked out for me. Lying on my bed was a red dress that I will have a pour myself into and tall red high heels. I debated between the pant suit that I picked out and the dress that Kage so gracefully picked out for me to wear. I heard sounds of people downstairs so I knew I had to hurry and get dressed before Kage returned to my door. I slide on the dress that fit every curve that I have. The back of the dress hung low on my back and a slit crawled close to my hips. I slide on the heels that made me even taller than my 5'9" frame. I let my hair fall out of the clip that held it up. The long black curls fell to my waist. I looked in the mirror to see how I looked. I didn't even recognize myself. I was extremely beautiful in red. I have to admit Kage has great taste. I opened the door and eased out in the hall. I stood at the top of the stairs to look over the crowd. I didn't see Kage anywhere. You would have thought he would be standing at the end of the stairs to laugh at me.

The whisper in my ear startled me. The voice told me that I look amazing. I smiled at Kage's voice but when I turned around I was face to face with Antonio.

"Thank you Antonio, have you seen Kage tonight?"

"Who cares about my brother? Why don't you let me show you around?" He took my hand and took me down stairs. When we got about half way down the stairs the crowd went silent like something just took their breath. I asked Antonio what was wrong. He told me that it was me that had caught everyone's breath. I felt my cheeks get hot. I finally got away from Antonio introducing to me everyone. I searched through the house for Kage and couldn't find him. I finally found him through the windows on the back patio. I opened the doors to the outside and found him standing looking up at the sky. I eased up behin him and whisper in his ear, "The stars are beautiful this time of night."

"They most certainly are, among other things." His smile melted my heart when I looked at him. "Ilayi, you are beautiful tonight. See, I told you that outfit would look better on you."

"And here I thought I was the one that decided what I was wearing." His laugh is so amazing. His whole face lights up. "Kage, I have an odd feeling about this part. Why did you not tell me on the plane that Antonio was your brother?"

"I didn't tell you because he is not really my brother, well not by birth anyway. I was adopted by his parents when I was three. I was always raised as his brother. We both carry the same last name but he is not my brother. I have always trusted him with my life but the last time I was here he was different somehow. This party of his gives me chills."

"Something is off about this party but I don't know what it is exactly. So if you wouldn't mind I would like to keep you as close as possible tonight."

"Oh I don't think that will be a problem" Kage said with a laugh.

"Hey, do you think we could find a place that's a little less freezing."

Kage smiled, "Sure, I think I can handle that. Come on inside and I will get us something to drink."

As we walked toward the bar I could feel someone watching me. I looked around the room to see who it was. A man with blonde hair standing in the other room against the huge window panes was staring at me. When he realizes that I was watching him he just smiles and nods his head toward me. Kage started me when he touched my arm. "Ilayi, are you okay? What's wrong? You look like you are scared to death."

"Kage, there is a man watching me from the other room."

"What? Where? Show me."

I turned around to show Kage the man and he was gone. "He was right there Kage, I swear."

"Ilayi, what did he look like?"

"He had blonde hair, silver eyes, and . . ."

"And what Ilayi?"

"He looked a hell of a lot like you, Kage. I think I am going to go to my room for awhile."

"Okay I will walk you up."

As we walked through the house I tried to find the man that scared Ilayi so bad. When we got to her quarters, she turned to me and smiled. It wasn't her normal smile that melted my heart, but a smile that told me that she was really scared of this man. "Ilayi, are you going to be alright tonight?"

"I'll be fine. I just need some rest from the long trip."

"Okay, I will be next door if you need me."

"Thank you again for the night of stars Kage."

"It was my pleasure to see so many things that are so beautiful tonight."

She leaned into me and kissed me on the check, "Good night Kage."

"Good night my lady of the stars."

When Ilayi closed and locked the door, I went back down the stairs to find this man that she was so afraid of. I stayed close to the walls in the shadows hoping to get a look at this man. I went from room to room and couldn't find him. I went outside and searched all the property. After making sure that everything was clear, I went to my room to think.

Chapter 11

The brothers were out on patrol for the night. They had widened their search hoping to find some reason for the killings. Craven and Devin are sitting near a club in one of the dark alleys watching what came from the club. Craven's skin was crawling on his body. The thoughts of Ilayi in her bed keep running through my head. I can still feel her next to me. I feel her skin touching mine. If it's like this now, how is it going to be if we ever exchange blood to be bonded forever? I guess I was in my own little world when Devin yelled at me, "Dude, what is the matter with you lately? You stand here like you're millions of miles away. You got in Marcus's face the other night over a girl. What the hell is going on with you? Whatever it is, you better get your shit together before you jump in Marcus's face like that again. Man, I know you and him go back further than any of us but that is no excuse. Bro, really, do we need to talk about something?"

"Devin, you really want to go there? I don't think that would be a good ideal right now."

"Whatever man, I am here when you need me okay? It's quite around here, let's get out of here for awhile."

The two brothers walked in Moonlights and saw that they weren't the only ones to give up on the search. Marcus was sitting in the VIP section already. When we set down at our table the waitress came by and asked what we wanted to drink. Devin ordered a beer and a woman like always. Craven ordered shots of Jack Daniels. Marcus just looked at him with a strange expression on his face. Devin got up and went to the downstairs dance floor to find women. He nestled up to a pretty blonde as soon as he got on the floor. Marcus said, "I will be glad if he grows up soon."

Craven looked at him with concern, "Devin will get there soon enough. He is already one hell of a fighter."

"Craven, we need to talk about something."

"Hell, I knew you would so just spit it out and let's get on with the night shall we?"

"So are you going to tell me what the hell is the problem with you or can I guess? I bet she has long black hair and she is sexy as hell. Am I getting close to your problem?"

"AH HELL! We had sex the other night so you know that puts me in a direct connection with her right?"

"Yeah I know that, so?"

"I don't know, I have been feeling all out of sort all day. I can't really explain it. I know something is wrong put I really can't place what it is. I hate having the same feelings that she has in our connection. Earlier tonight she was scared and I got pissed off for nothing."

"Scared! What do you mean scared, Craven?"

"I don't know it's just a feeling that something was wrong with her. Has Tate heard anything from them two anyways?"

"I don't think so, maybe we should get Tate on the phone now. At least you will calm down some. I have never seen you jump in my face like you did yesterday."

"Marcus, I told you nothing is wrong, put the damn phone down."

Devin walked up to the table then. "Wow! What the fuck is with you two these days."

"Man, fuck both of you. I'm out of here."

"Craven wait man, we need to talk about this."

"Devin let him go. He will cool off and go back to the compound later."

Devin set down and downed Craven's shots of jack. "Damn, that warms the body up. So Marcus, what is going on with him?

He's looked like hell the past couple of days, ever since that woman left. I know he slept with her, the lucky bastard. You can smell it all over him. Craven sleeps with a lot of women so what the hell is up with this one?"

Marcus looked at Devin with a slight grin. "Oh Hell!!! You got to be kidding me. She is Craven's blood mark?"

"I didn't say that Devin, but I think it's a possibility."

Craven steps out into the cool night air. A man bumped his shoulder when he stepped off the last step of the club. "Man what the fuck is your problem?"

"Sorry man, I didn't see you there." When he turned, their eyes met. Craven had a feeling that he should know this guy but it was Ilayi's feelings, not his. That pissed Craven off knowing that his blood mark had been with this guy. He turned away from the guy before he went off on him.

As he walked down the sidewalk, Dalton stared at him. He knows what Craven is. He thought about following him and killing him but he decided to go inside the club to cool off. Craven felt someone staring at him. When he turned around, Dalton's eyes were a bright blue as he turned to go inside the club. Craven had a feeling that he couldn't shake. His body was on fire from the inside out. His blood was boiling in his veins. He saw a park nearby and he headed to it to sit down. He sat down on the bench to get his breath. What the hell is going on with me? The taste of blood came in his mouth. Damn! I got to get to the compound. He got his phone opened and dialed Devin's number.

"Hello Craven, what's up?"

"Devin I'm taking the SUV back to the compound."

"Okay man, I will catch a ride from Marcus."

Craven got to the compound and headed straight to the control room. "Tate, have you heard from Kage and Ilayi yet?"

Tate was on the phone when Craven busted in the room. He raised a hand to shut Craven up for a minute. "Okay Kage, I understand. Call me at night fall tomorrow night to update me more. I will be waiting for your call." Then he hung up the phone.

He turned to Craven to see he was breathing hard leaning up against his desk. "Was that Kage on the phone? Is everything alright there? Is Ilayi safe?"

"Damn Craven, one at a time please. Yes that was Kage on the phone. There has been a development there that he is checking on. And yes! Ilayi is in her room safe. Now tell me what the hell is wrong with you."

"Are you sure she is safe?"

"Yes, Kage said she had a headache and was lying down in her room. Now tell me what the hell is wrong for you to bust up in here."

"I feel that she is scared about something."

"Craven, there is only one way you could feel her feelings. Damn Craven! You slept with her didn't you? Did you trade blood with her too?"

"Don't be a smartass Tate. No, I didn't trade blood with her. Do you think I'm stupid to make her mine forever?"

"Kage is suppose to call me back tomorrow night so just wait until then. I'm sure if anything is wrong, Kage will let me know okay? He can take care of her over there Craven."

Chapter 12

I leaned against the door after Kage left. Who was that man downstairs? I have never seen him before and yet it seems like I should know him from my past. It was hard to convince Kage that I was alright when he walked away from my room. I could tell that he didn't want to leave me alone. Why was I so damn scared of this man? Maybe with some rest I will think better in morning. I changed into some yoga pants and a tank to sleep in. It's not my usual sleeping gear. I slide between the satin sheets and sigh. The sheets were cool against my skin. I rolled and tumbled in the bed trying to get comfortable. My body is still shaken by that man. I listen to the sounds around the house and finally fell off to sleep.

I woke up with someone's hands over my mouth. I struggled trying to get away but I couldn't. My hands and feet had been tied together. There is something that is covering my head and face. I can hear men talking to each other. I don't know the voices. Wait!! Is that Antonio's voice I hear? Why is he not helping me? He is telling the other men to take me somewhere. I can't hear where it is that they are taking me. Panic stirs in my stomach. They know who I am. I have to get out of here. I can't let them take me but how can I stop them? I can't scream to let Kage know. Let me think! *Craven!*

He can sense me. He told me that we would always be connected. Okay. So how do I get to Craven? I close my eyes and think of him. I can feel that they are moving me somewhere. I squirm trying to get loose.

"Hold her tighter! You can't let her get away from you. Hurry you idiots, before someone sees you. Go out the back, there is a van waiting on you there. Call me when you arrive at the cabin and I can give you more instructions then. Make sure you contain her properly. She is a fighter. She is the ticket for our redemption."

Ilayi's heart was pounding so loud it hurt her ears. She was so scared that she was almost sick to her stomach. Her head hurt from the drugs that they gave her. What am I going to do? I can't let them get my blood. There will be nothing left of the brotherhood if they get it. They will rule the world of vampires. The humans will be feasted upon. Innocent people dying for nothing. I have to stop this from happening.

The ride was long. We had been traveling for about three hours I guess when we came to a stop. This is it. This is the place where I will die. I should never have gone to the brotherhood. I should have stayed hidden like I had been for centuries. I heard the van cut off and doors starting to open. If I have a chance of escaping I will have to do it when they come for me. I rolled over and got in position to kick whoever opened the door. Maybe I can distract them long enough to get away. The doors flew open and I was about to kick when I saw him. It was Dalton but how? It can't be. Damn, how could I have been so stupid? My heart broke in to pieces. He had betrayed me. After all this time, he is a crone. How could I not have seen it? His deep blue eyes burned me to the core.

"Ilayi, you look surprised to see me." The smile that crossed his face was pure evil. "I gave you every chance to see what I was. I knew who you were when I moved in that apartment. You are my treasure that I will use to prove that I should be the leader of the crones. Then you left for a few days and I got worried that you had run to the brotherhood. When I ran into your male at the club the other night I knew that you had been with him. He carried the mark of you and you carry the mark of him. I thought I would teach him a lesson that night but I decided to let him suffer in the pain of your death instead. The death of blood mates is extremely painful. It will eat at you until you are mad. I think that Craven won't have that problem. When this is over and I have stolen all your blood, my crones will be able to hunt during the day. I will seek their compound and kill every one of the brotherhood members in their sleep. Then I will be the ruler of the world."

My mind was running overtime. If what he is telling me is true then Craven really was my blood mate. How is that possible? I thought it was just a sexual attraction thing with him. If I am Craven's mate then I am truly connected to him. My heart ached to find him. I screamed at Dalton in rage, "You will never get the chance to bleed me dry. I will be coming for you and I will kill you myself!"

The hand that hit my face was hard and powerful. I tasted blood in my mouth and saw stars in front of me. Then everything turned black.

Chapter 13

We were all sitting in the control room discussing the deaths. Tate was at the computers searching to see if we had overlooked anything. Devin was stretched across the couch arguing with Tate that there has to be something else in the police files. Marcus was pacing the floor like he always does when he is thinking of a plan. I was standing against the wall looking and listening to the situation. My skin still tingled from the previous night. I got a pain in my stomach that dropped me to my knees when the phone rang. "Craven, what the hell is happening to you?"

Marcus turned around to see that I was on the floor. "Craven, what is going on?"

"It's not me Marcus. It's through my bond. Ilayi is in trouble."

I heard Tate on the phone. He was talking to Kage in England. "Okay Kage, let me put you on the speaker phone so that the team can hear you also. Okay, go ahead."

"Hey guys look, I have some bad news to tell you but I am on the situation."

Marcus said, "What is the problem Kage?"

"I went to check on Ilayi tonight after I came back from checking the property. There was a guy at the party last night that scared the hell out of her. I was trying to find him. When I got back and knocked on her door..."

"She is gone from the mansion!" Craven screamed out loud.

"Yes she was gone when I broke the door in. There had been a struggle there. I know that she would not go without a fight guys."

"Marcus, she is hurting bad. She is being tortured somehow."

"Tate, find us away there now. Kage, do what you can there. We are on our way to you."

"Marcus I'm sorry, I know it was my job to protect her."

"It's alright Kage, you just have me some answers when I get there." The phone hung up and everyone was talking at once.

I felt myself blacking out then I felt hands on me. In the blackness I could feel Ilayi trying to get to me. She is so scared. I can feel her getting weak. I hear her calling my name. I can't find her though. I scream with rage because I can't get to her. She is hurting so much. I woke up screaming. Marcus put his hands on my shoulders. "There you are man. You have been out for a while."

"Marcus, they are hurting her. She is getting weak."

"I know Craven, I have been here all night with you man."

"Tate got us a ride there yet?"

"Yes, we leave in about an hour but I think that you shouldn't go Craven."

"Fuck you Marcus, I'm going with you and there is nothing that you can do to stop me. She is my blood mate and I know that now."

"Are you sure that you can handle this?"

"Lets just get there and I will show you that I can handle this. I am going to rip whoever took her to shreds."

"I thought you might, so lets get things ready."

The brothers meet in the control room to get things ready for the trip. "Tate, have you heard anything from Kage yet?"

"Yeah, he said that he would meet us at the airport with some information."

"Marcus, I'm going with you."

"No you're not. I need you here to protect the compound while we are gone. You are my best defense here. I need someone here if something happens and we don't get back."

"The plane will pick you up at 9pm and you will arrive at the other airport around 4am. That will give you enough time to get to the mansion before the sun comes up."

Ilayi woke up smelling flesh burning. When she opened her eyes she realized it was her that she smelled. She was hanging from a chain that was cutting into her skin. She saw blood dripping in a container. She looked around the room and saw that it was daylight through the glass ceiling above her. She must have been here for hours. She is weak from the sun and the loss of blood.

Her head hurt extremely from not feeding. The door opened and Dalton came in the room. He stayed in the shadow until the ceiling was covered with shields. She took a deep breath and smelled his intense power.

He moved toward me like a panther on the prowl. The muscles in his body moved with power. His blue eyes were magical. He was like looking at the depths of the ocean. They always took my breath away when he came to my apartment. I still can feel his touch on my body. How could I have been so stupid about him? I see now that he looks and acts like a predator and nothing else. He touched my face with his hand and I spit in his face. Well that cost me a hit in the face. He busted my lip with that one.

"Aww! Ilayi, be my mate and I will stop all of this punishment. I will give you anything you want. You could be my queen over the crones."

"That will never happen in this life time and you know it."

"We could have all the power in the world in our hands, together."

My heart broke in two just hearing his voice. He betrayed me though and for that I will kill him the first chance I get.

"I will check back with you later to see if you are still breathing." He laughed at that. He turned when he opened the door, "Oh, by the way, I will tell Craven for you right before I kill him."

I screamed at Dalton as he shut the door. The shields opened again and I could feel the heat on my skin. I screamed from the burning of the sun.

Chapter 14

There was a black SUV waiting when we landed at the airport. Marcus opened the door of the airplane. Kage got out of the SUV and came toward us. There was another male that was behind Kage. He was tall and had dark hair that went to his shoulders. His eyes were dark gray, almost black. His presence gave you the feeling that he has a lot of secrets. I guess we will know when Marcus touches him.

Kage was on edge when the brothers came out the plane. They had never known anything about this part of his life. He had always kept things that were about his family from them. He took Marcus's hand and the others. "Marcus, this is my brother Antonio."

Marcus looked at him with surprise, "Your brother?"

"Antonio this is Marcus, the leader of the Marked Brotherhood, and this is Craven and Devin."

"The pleasure is all mine."

Marcus thought something was strange about this male. He really couldn't put his finger on it. As they walked toward the SUV, Marcus and Craven stopped and turned to see half a dozen crones behind them. All their fangs came out at once and they were ready for battle. The crones charged at them and their silver blades came out with vengeance. Craven started slicing at one crone and cut one of them against the chest. Black blood ran from his chest. The crone screamed and charged at Craven again. Craven was ready for him and sliced his head off. Craven turned to see what was happening to the other brothers. They were holding their own pretty well. Craven saw that Marcus had two on him so he ran to get one of the crones off of him. He grabbed the crone that was on Marcus's back. The crone hissed at Craven and came at him. The crone cut Craven across the arm. Craven went after the crone and sliced him across his back. The crone screamed with pain. He turned just as Craven got him again with his sword. Craven sliced the crone across his stomach and the crone dropped in front of him. The crone was pleading to him to spare him. Craven started to take the crone's head when a pain hit him and dropped him to his knees. Kage saw Craven fall to the ground. He turned and took the crone's head that he was fighting and ran to Craven. Kage leaped over Craven's back and took the crone's head that he was fighting in front of him. Craven screamed in terror. Kage caught his arm and held him up.

When all the crones were dead, Marcus turned to hear Craven yell out with terror. "Get him to the fucking SUV now! Devin, you watch our backs."

Devin turned to see if there was any sign of crones. He watched as they got Craven in the SUV safely. The other brothers ran and got in the SUV.

"Antonio, we need the fastest way to your compound now." Antonio looked at the driver and then the SUV took off fast. "Marcus, what the hell is wrong with him?"

"Craven is linked to Ilayi."

Kage looked at Marcus with concern and then turned to Craven. "You linked yourself to Ilayi?"

"Do you have information to find her?"

Kage turned to Marcus and said "You're not going to like this. The crones have her I know for sure. They have a new male with them that does not have a scent to track."

"What do you mean this male has no scent to him? How in the hell can we track them then to find Ilayi?"

"I can track her if she is close enough" said Craven. "I could feel her when I was in the states, so I don't think it will be hard to find her here. She is being extremely tortured wherever she is. She is in so much damn pain. When I find this male that has her, I am going to rip his fucking head off."

"Craven, we will find her."

Antonio was sitting in the front seat of the SUV grinning that they didn't have a clue where she was and that he was the one that had taken her. He didn't think that it would be this easy after all of these years of trying to find her location. His plan couldn't have been working any better. He had the pure one, Ilayi, and he had the brotherhood all in one place to kill. He had to actually laugh to his self.

Chapter 15

Ilayi woke up again to the feel of a knife going across her arm. She screamed in pain. "You son of a bitch, you will pay for this I swear."

Dalton just smiled at her and said, "I doubt that will happen. You see my darling, your so called brotherhood has been killed by now so there is no one coming for you. I am going to bleed you slowly. I want you to suffer like I have all of these years."

"What in the hell are you talking about? How would you know anything about suffering? You're nothing but a rich, spoiled brat."

"That is what I wanted you to think. You really don't remember do you Ilayi?"

"What am I suppose to remember Dalton? That you are nothing but a liar, cheater, and a betrayer?"

"Ilayi, remember the night your parents were killed?" He pulled his self close to her face. He whispered beside her ear. "You remember your father killed my father in the middle of the court that night. My family was torn apart for what your father did that night. My mother wouldn't even look at me. My father came for me that night in the bar. I use to be a drunk of sorts." His fangs drop for her to see what he was. "I was the one that came for your parents that night. I was the one that killed them for the revenge of my father."

Ilayi's eyes widen, "You're the one that killed my parents?"

"I came back that night to search for you but you were already gone. It has taken me all these years to find you. Now that I have, it will be a pleasure to give you a slow death."

The blood was dripping from my arm. Hot tears ran down my face at the news of my parents' murder. Dalton turned and left the room laughing. The sun was down and all the stars were out tonight. I closed my eyes to search for Craven. What will I do now that Craven is gone too? I will die here in this cabin. The tears burned my skin as they reached my burns. Images of my parents came to me in a dream. I could see Craven's face there with my parents.

When we got to the compound I was on the verge of blacking out again. I can't stand Ilayi suffering. She is going through so much and we are all standing around here trying to figure out what is the best way to find her. I know the best way. That is to follow my heart. It will lead me straight to her. Our souls have to bring us together again. It has to be enough. I go upstairs to Ilayi's bedroom to see if I can find anything to lead me to her. Her being tortured is killing me. I shut the door behind me and lock the door so that the other brothers are not all in my business. I knew that they wouldn't understand if I had the guts to come out and tell them that I am in love with Ilayi. They would think that I have gone soft but I am on the verge of killing something. The room was a mess. The bed looks like she was took in her sleep. The sheets are messed up for her. The night that we spent together she slept so still in one place. There had been a struggle here for sure. I can feel my anger grow even stronger from her scent of warm vanilla skin. I look around to see if anything was missing. Her knife is still on the dresser where I guess she left it. She didn't even have a chance to defend herself. The rage is building inside me like a volcano. I lie on her bed to think. Her smell overwhelms me. My fangs extend out of rage. I close my eyes and I see her beautiful face. I can see her long black hair draping us while she is on top of me. I can still feel her touch on my skin. The images keep coming to me. Her standing on the sidewalk with her knives in my face. The way she looked at me in the hall of the compound. I took a deep breath just as a pain hit my arm. I grit my teeth to handle the pain. I know it comes from her and it makes me want to rip someone to pieces. A picture of a room with open ceilings comes to me. It's dark when I look around and I am pleased that I am alone. Where is this coming from? Oh Fuck! I'm looking through Ilayi. The door opened and a male came through the door. She had mixed feeling about this male. I have seen this male before. Oh Shit! It's the guy from the club the other night. The one that bumped into my arm outside the club. He came closer to her. He touched her face and she moved from his hand. He drew back and hit her, then the connection was gone. I jumped up and yanked the door open to run downstairs and ran into Marcus. "Damn it! Marcus what are you doing here? First, I have information on Ilayi." Marcus called everyone downstairs into the study. "She is in a room with open ceilings. It looks like a cabin or something. She has marks that look like burns, probably from the open ceiling. The crone that has her she knows well. They had a connection. Marcus, it's the guy that bumped into me outside the club the other night. I knew I should have torn him apart that night. She is weak too, Marcus. I don't know how much longer she can hold out. I sensed that she had lost blood."

Marcus paced the floor. "Kage, you said that this vampire has no scent."

"Yeah, that's what I've been told around here. That is probably why I couldn't get a track on him the other night at the party."

"Craven look at me!"

Craven turned to Marcus with his fangs extended. "That son of a bitch is torturing her to death. I cannot allow that any longer."

"I know Craven but we have to wait until dark. We can't be running out there now frying our asses. We are no good to her dead. We need to get some rest and meet back here at dusk. That goes for everyone. Antonio, do you have some rooms that we can borrow?"

Antonio stepped out from the door toward the bothers. "I will have the butler get them ready right away." He yelled for the butler and he came to the door of the study. "Raymond, I need rooms for my friends and please make it quick."

"Yes Sir, I will return in a few minutes."

"Thank you Raymond."

Chapter 16

I could feel Craven with me through out connection. I hope that I showed him enough to maybe find me. God! I hope he comes soon. I don't know how much longer I can hold on. I feel my body getting weaker. I'm losing blood too fast now with the new cut across my arm. I guess I should try to sleep while the sun is down. My skin is not healing like it should from the lack of blood in my body. I don't think that I can take another day of being burned like this. My body is going to give out before I do. I close my eyes and dream of Craven. Could we really have a future together before all of this? Would he be willing to except me as someone equal to him? I see him with the brotherhood being so strong for them. He is a true warrior. Then I see him in my room so soft and gentle with me but yet so strong in his body with every move. He slips into my thoughts again. I have never had a bond with someone this strong. Is this the work of the blood mate? It makes us feel as one. I wish I could have the chance to be bonded to Craven. I want to spend the rest of my life with this brother.

I feel my body weaken even more. I keep blacking out from the loss of blood. I know that it won't be long now, maybe a few hours left of my life. I wish I could see him one last time to tell him how I feel.

Back at the compound Craven is restless. He hates having to wait until dark to go after her. He is lying on her bed trying to sort out all the emotions that she is sending through the bond. I feel her love toward something. I feel her strength fading more. I feel her fear of dying. These feelings are killing me. I get up and go downstairs heading to the gym to work out some of this stress. I hear voices downstairs somewhere. I can tell one of them is Antonio. He is arguing with someone. I ease downstairs toward the kitchen. I stand there listening through the door. I hear Ilayi's name and bust through the door. I see Antonio talking to...

"What the fuck are you doing here?" The blonde headed guy that hit my shoulder at the club that night was standing there. Antonio said he was a friend. My eyes narrow and my fangs come out. His eyes were amber in a second. I smell Ilayi's fear on him. This was the man that I saw hit her across the face. I flew and hit him against the door. I held him off the floor with his throat. "Where in the hell is she? You need to tell me now!"

"Dude, I don't know what you are talking about."

The door flew open and the rest of the brothers were standing there ready for battle. "Craven what in the fuck are you doing?"

"Marcus, I smell her fear on him. This little fucker is the one that I saw hit her through our bond."

All their fangs came out. Their eyes changed to amber. Kage looked at Antonio with confusion.

"I heard them talking about Ilayi. He has her and she is drawing weaker."

Kage struck Antonio across the face. "You knew about this? Are you the one that got her out of the house?"

Antonio smiled, "Kage, you wouldn't understand. She has the blood that can make you and me into day walkers. Imagine what we could accomplish during the day. We could hunt and feed when we wanted to." Antonio threw Kage against the wall. Kage got Antonio across the neck with his knife. Antonio fell to the floor in two pieces.

Kage was standing over his body with his head low. "Craven man, I am so sorry. I didn't know. I would have never brought her here if I knew."

"The only chance you have here is to tell me where in the fuck she is." Craven had a knife held to Dalton's throat.

"You will never find her in time and you know it."

Craven dug the knife into his neck. Dalton screamed out with pain. "I said tell me where she is now."

"She is in a cabin off of 241 in the forest." Dalton laughed, "She will be dead when you get there."

Craven turned and sliced him through his neck. Dalton fell to the floor.

The three hours to dusk was something that I couldn't bear. I felt her life slipping away. We were all in the study planning how to get in the cabin. We know that we will have to fight our way inside to her. I can't even think straight. My heart is breaking standing here knowing that I will not get to her in time. The sun is setting and I can't wait any longer. I turn around to see that the brothers were watching me. "I have to go to her now with or without you."

The other brothers smiled at him and headed toward the door. I know that my brothers will stand and fight to the death with me to get to her. Kage turned toward the kitchen.

"Kage, where are you going?"

He turned around and said "I have one last thing to do here."

Marcus laid a strong hand on his shoulder, "We will wait for you in the car."

Craven saw the hurt and despair in his face. He looked up at Craven, "Craven, give me a few minutes and then we will go get that female of yours out of that shitvhole she's in." Kage turned back to the kitchen. The rest of the brothers headed outside. In less than five minutes, Kage came out and got in the car. "Marcus, we need to leave now, like right now. I left a little gift for my dear brother's compound." A grin crossed Kage's face. Marcus slammed on the gas. They got to the end of the drive when the fireworks lit up behind them. Kage just grinned now, "Lets get to the fighting."

Chapter 17

Everyone was quite on the way to the cabin. Everyone was in their own mind replaying their strategy. Everyone's emotions were everywhere. To my brothers we are saving the pure vampire Ilayi. To me I am trying to keep from raging out of terror that I might be too late for her. This female is my true blood mate and she is the pure vampire among us. The first of her kind in five thousand years to be born. I sit here trying to get a position on her emotions. I can't detect her now. I really hope that she is still breathing. My body and soul feels like it has been ripped from me.

We park about a mile from the cabin so that we can't be detected if there are more vampires in the cabin. Marcus looked at all of us with an expression full of emotions. "Brothers, I don't know what we will find when we get in there. If by chance we are too late for Ilayi, we will still bring her with us for a proper burial." All the brothers hung their heads in approval. "Craven, my brother, I don't know what kind of shape she will be in. You know that we will all protect you and your blood mate with our lives."

The other guys were mumbling but all I could do was think about her. The rage built up in me from somewhere inside. I have never had this much rage within me.

"Okay Kage, I want you to get around to the back of the cabin. Devin, I want you on the left side coming in from the woods. Craven, I want you to be on the other side coming in from the lake. I will go in front so that they can detect me and focus on me."

Everyone nodded in approval and we headed toward the house. Kage diminished in the back. Devin and I took our places by the cabin. I could see Marcus in the front of the cabin. The door opened and I knew they had found him. A very weak emotion grabbed me. It's her, she's not in the house. Where is she then? I looked around again and saw a small building about two yards on the other side of the lake. Her presence was stronger there. I yanked the door off the building. Two vampires attacked me at once. I took my knives out to attack. One of the vampires caught my arm with a sword. My rage was so high seeing her hanging there that I could not control it. The next thing I knew I was standing in front of her with tears running down my face and the two vampires were on the floor at her feet.

"Ilayi, can you hear me?" She didn't move to my voice. I found the end of the chains and lowered her to the floor. I could still hear the fighting of my brothers from outside. I laid her head in my lap. I couldn't see her breathing. "Please Ilayi, don't leave me." I felt for a pulse. It was very weak but she was alive. Her body was burned from head to toe. I saw the cuts on her wrist and arm. I kissed them softly to close them up. She had lost so much blood. I heard someone enter the doorway. I was ready to defend her with my life and then I saw that it was the brothers. The look on their face told me that it was as bad as I thought.

"Marcus, we need to get her somewhere. She is alive but barely."

Kage said "I know a place not to far from here. Lets get her in the SUV."

They came in to help carry her but I wouldn't allow it. "I have her, just make sure we get there fast."

Craven placed his hands gently under her and picked her up next to his chest. They moved to the SUV quickly. They were on the road within minutes.

"Marcus, there is a place just up there on the right."

Marcus turned into a driveway with pavement. It circled around to the back of a huge house. He turned the ignition and lights off.

Kage said "Give me a minute and I will let you in." Within minutes Kage opened the door to let them in the compound.

"There is a room up the stairs on the left ready for her, Craven." Craven nodded with a thank you.

I carried her up the stairs to the room. There was a huge bed of black satin in the room. I laid her down on the bed. She moaned a little and I had to smile. I lay down beside her and held her close to me. "Ilayi, I need you to drink from me. Ilayi, can you hear me? I have you and your safe now."

She whispered his name. Craven bit his wrist and put it to her mouth.

"Ilayi, drink please."

He let his blood drip into her mouth. She swallowed after a few minutes of coaching. He put his wrist to her mouth and she drank from it with intention. The burning of their bonding hurt his veins but he didn't stop. He knew that from now on that he would always be linked to her, forever. He saw that she was trying to heal. She opened her eyes and pushed his arm away from her mouth.

"Ilayi, you have to drink more. You need more."

She started to say something and he stopped her with his wrist against her mouth. She knew it was no use in arguing with him so she drank more from him.

When she had enough, I pulled away from her. Her eyes burned with amber. Her burns had healed with my blood. The cuts were almost all gone. She looked so small against me. She is so beautiful.

"You linked me to you forever Craven." The look in her eyes was sad.

He pulled her to him and buried his face in her hair. "I had to save you. I could not ever loose you. Ilayi, I love you forever. You are my true blood mate if you will have me."

She whispered his name in his chest and it sent shivers over his body. "Craven I love you with all that I have."

He pulled her back from him and she grinned, sending him over the top. He kissed her gently. "I am going to start the water for a hot shower to make you feel better okay?' He got off the bed and went into the bathroom.

I could hear the water starting in the shower. He came back and lifted me off the bed and carried me into the bathroom. He stood me in front of him and started to undress me. It was so beautiful how gentle he was with me. I felt his hands easing over my body. He was sizzling my skin with his touch. I want him so bad against me. I want him to hold me and caress me with his strong hands. I stepped into the shower and let the water run over my body. I could sense that he was still watching me through the glass door. The urge of wanting him was getting stronger with every minute. I showered and washed my hair. I turn the water off and slide the door open expecting to see Craven still standing there. I took the towel and wrapped it around me. I went into the bedroom and there was still no sign of him. Just then the door opened and he came in with clothes in his hands. He just smiled when he saw me standing there.

"I thought I would get you something to wear since you didn't have anything on when I found you."

She grinned and dropped her towel to the floor. "Craven, I don't think that I want them just right yet."

He smiled and threw the clothes on the dresser. He came and stood in front of her. He placed his hands on the sides of her face and kissed her softly. She slid her hands under his shirt and rubbed her hands over his smooth skin. He moaned to the touch her hands. She slid the shirt over his head. He caught her mouth again with his. She pulled away and kissed his chin line down his neck to his chest to find his nipple. She flicked it with her tongue and he moaned out loud. His hands were in her hair. She moved over to catch the other nipple with her tongue. He shivered a little under her and she had to smile. She moved to his stomach kissing and nibbling it, working her way down to his jeans that he had changed into. She undid his jeans and dropped them to the floor. She smiled at the huge bulge in front of her. She moaned a little then and it sent him over the edge. She slid his boxers off to the floor. She took a hold of his manhood with her hands and stroked it. She then took his whole manhood in her mouth sliding down his shaft. She grabbed his balls with the other hand and squeezed a little. He moaned loudly and she knew he was pleased with what she was doing. After a few minutes of that, he couldn't hold out much longer. He grabbed her up and placed her on the bed. He placed his hands on her thighs caressing them gently. He kissed her inner thigh and she couldn't help but moan. He slides up to her core flicking his tongue on her clit. She puts her hands in his hair to hold on. Her body shivers with what he is doing to her. She feels her orgasm building with every stroke of his tongue on her core. He slides two fingers into her wetness. She barely held on to herself. He felt her move her hips to his mouth. He knew she was close to climaxing. He wanted to taste every inch of her. Her body shook with the orgasm when it released from her body. He savored every inch of her orgasm. She tried to pull away but he held onto her hips so that she could ride her orgasm all the way through. When she was through with her orgasm, he rose to her nipples and took them into his mouth and sucked on them making her shiver all over her body. He reached to her mouth and saw that she had transformed. Her fangs were out and her eyes were beautiful amber. He had to smile that he had pleased her so well. He showed his fangs to her and she smiled. "I want you inside me Craven, now." She didn't have to ask twice. I slid my manhood into her wetness. She was so tight that I had to work a little into her at a time. When I got all of it in her, I drove it deep inside her. She gasped for air with a moan. I moved slowly so that she could get use to me. Her walls were so damn tight around me that I thought I would lose it immediately. I held on for awhile moving slowly in her. She dug into my back with her sharp nails and I had to moan. That almost sent me over the edge. "Craven, bite me so that we will be completed bonded together." Craven looked into her eyes, "You don't have to do that Ilayi."

"I know, but I want you to. I want to be with you forever as one." She tilted her head to one side and her veins were so vivid. "Ilayi, you are still weak. I can't do that right now to you."

"Craven take me now, my soul and body. Take it now!!!"

He leaned down and licked her neck and bit down into her artery. She moaned loudly. Her blood is rich and strong. I can feel it changing me somehow. I know now what made her so special to the vampires. Her blood is so rich. She moaned and her body shook. That sent me over the edge right away. We both moaned out loud when the orgasm came to both of us at the same time. We both collapsed on the bed beside each other. I held her in my arms tightly. "We will now be together forever. Our love with conquer everything."

www.ingramcontent.com/pod-product-compliance
Lightning Source LLC
LaVergne TN
LVHW040201080526
838202LV00042B/3267